The Snake who Came to Stay

The Snake who Came to Stay

Julia Donaldson

Illustrated by
Hannah Shaw

Barrington Stoke

First published in 2012 in Great Britain by
Barrington Stoke Ltd
18 Walker Street, Edinburgh, EH3 7LP

www.barringtonstoke.co.uk

This edition first published 2016

Text © 2012 Julia Donaldson
Illustrations © 2012 Hannah Shaw

Colouring by Catriona Black

A CIP catalogue record for this book is available
from the British Library upon request

ISBN: 978-1-78112-574-8

Printed in China by Leo

This book is super readable for young readers beginning
their independent reading journey.

To everyone at Miltonbank Primary School

Contents

Chapter 1
Holidays for Pets

"A snake?" said Mum. "A snake? No, you're not looking after a snake."

"Oh, please, Mum," said Polly. "It's only for the holidays."

Polly knew what Mum was like. Sometimes "No" could turn into "I'll think about it".

"Doris is a very nice snake," said
Polly. "I've met her. She's not poisonous.
Oh, don't be mean, Mum!"

"Mean!" said Mum. "What a cheek!
I've said yes to two guinea pigs, a bird
and a whole lot of goldfish! I just don't
fancy a snake in the house."

"But where else can Doris go?" asked Polly. "She can't go on holiday with Jack. And we're not going away. Oh, go on, Mum!"

"Well ..." said Mum. "I'll think about it. But I want you to take that notice down from the front gate."

The notice on the gate said –

POLLY'S HOLIDAY HOME

Holidays for Pets

Are you going away this summer?

Why not give your pets a holiday too?

Please phone 236566

Polly smiled as she took the notice down. She knew Mum. "I'll think about it" almost always meant "Yes".

Chapter 2
The Silent Snake

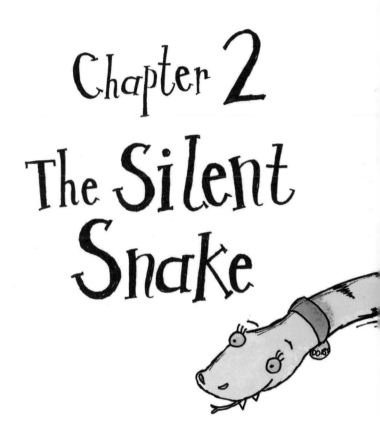

The first animals to arrive at Polly's Holiday Home were the two guinea pigs. They belonged to Polly's friend Katie and their names were Bill and Ben. Bill was thin and Ben was fat. They had their own house and garden. The house was called a hutch and the garden was called a run – it was a box made of wire netting which went on the grass.

Mum was happy when she saw how fast Bill and Ben ate the grass. "If we move their run every day I won't need to get the lawn mower out all summer," she said.

Bill and Ben needed extra food as well as the grass. When they were hungry they pushed their noses up to the wire netting and went, "Oooeeek! Oooeeek! Oooeeek!" They made so much noise that you could hear them from the house.

A few days after Bill and Ben came, Mrs McNair from down the road brought her big black mynah bird round. "He likes to be in the kitchen so he can join in all the talk, don't you, Charlie?" she said.

"Ding dong," said Charlie. He sounded just like a door bell.

"Charlie copies everything, don't you, Charlie?" said Mrs McNair.

Charlie put his head on one side.
Then he started to sing in a funny high
voice. "I dream of Jeannie with the light
brown hair," he sang.

Mrs McNair laughed. "He's copying me now. That's my favourite song, isn't it, Charlie?"

"Bbrm bbrm," said Charlie. Now he sounded just like a motor bike.

The goldfish didn't come to the Holiday Home, because they were in a pond in the garden next door. Polly just had to check on them and put more water in the pond if it didn't rain.

.

Doris the snake was the last animal to arrive. Jack brought her round in her tank. The tank had a little heater in it.

"But you still need to keep her in the warmest room in the house," said Jack.

"That's the kitchen," said Mum, with a sigh. "I won't have any space left to cook!"

But Mum did find a place for Doris on the worktop, between Charlie's cage and the phone.

"Goodbye, Doris," said Jack.

Doris didn't move. She didn't even hiss.

"You see, Mum?" said Polly. "She'll be no bother at all."

Chapter 3

The Copy Bird

The Holiday Home was a bit noisy for
Mum. Bill and Ben went, "Oooeeek!
Oooeeek!" and Charlie kept singing about
Jeannie with the light brown hair.

   And the phone rang all the time.
More and more people wanted to know if
Polly could look after their pets.

Mum always said "No", and Polly
didn't even try to turn it into "I'll think
about it".

But Doris the snake wasn't noisy at
all. Sometimes she hissed – but only
very softly.

"I told you she'd be good," said Polly.

One day Polly and Mum were having breakfast when the phone went yet again. Mum gave a sigh.

"I'll get it," said Polly. She picked up the phone and said hello, but there was no one there.

Then they heard the ringing noise again. "Bbrring-bbrring, bbrring-bbrring."

It was Charlie.

Polly laughed, but Mum said, "I'm not having that!" and she moved Charlie's cage into the sitting room.

Later that day, Polly was outside with the guinea pigs when the postman came with two postcards for her. One of the cards was from Mrs McNair. It had a picture of a Spanish dancer in a pretty

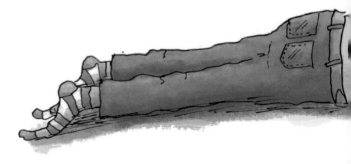

dress. Polly took it into the sitting room and showed it to Charlie. He looked at the girl on the front and said, "Pretty boy!"

The other card was from Jack. It had a picture of a vulture on it. On the back it said, "Show Doris this picture and tell her I miss her."

Polly went into the kitchen. She slid the top off Doris's tank and put the card in. Doris gave a soft hiss.

At the same time Polly heard an extra loud "Oooeeek! Oooeeek!" noise.

"It's those guinea pigs," she said.
"But they can't be hungry – I've just fed
them. I hope nothing's wrong."

Polly ran back outside. Bill and Ben
were in their run, eating the grass.

"That's funny!" said Polly.

Then she heard the noise again.
"Oooeeek! Oooeeek!" It was coming
from inside the house.

Polly went back to the house, into the
sitting room. There was Charlie, with
his head on one side, going, "Oooeeek!
Oooeeek! OOOEEEK!" just like Bill and
Ben.

Oooeeek!
Oooeeek!

"You copy cat," Polly said.

"I dream of Jeannie with the light brown hair," Charlie sang.

All at once, Polly remembered something. She stopped laughing. She had been in such a rush to check that the guinea pigs were all right that she'd left the top off Doris's tank!

"But Doris wouldn't escape," she said. "She's such a good, quiet, still kind of snake."

All the same, Polly ran back to the kitchen.

The tank was empty. Doris had gone.

Chapter 4

The Search

"She can't have gone far," said Polly. She
looked all round the room – in the sink,
because she knew snakes like water, and
under the radiator because they like to
keep warm.

No Doris.

Polly even looked under the cooker. Just then Mum came in. "What are you doing?" she asked.

"I'm looking for Doris," said Polly in a very small voice.

She knew what was coming next, and here it came.

"I said we shouldn't have a snake," shouted Mum. "I should never have said yes!"

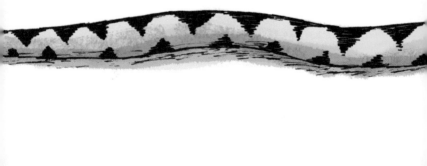

Mum did help Polly look for Doris, but every now and then she said something like, "What if she turns up in my bed in the middle of the night?" – which wasn't very helpful.

It was bad enough that Mum was cross, but it was Jack that Polly was really worried about. She knew he

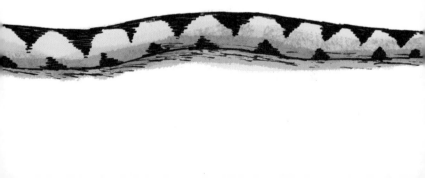

was missing Doris – he'd said so on his postcard. How was he going to feel if she was gone for ever?

Polly and Mum looked all over the house.

Mum had calmed down a bit.

"Well, it's very odd," she said, "but I'm sure she'll turn up. Leave the lid off the tank and put some food in it."

But the days passed and Doris didn't turn up. Polly felt sick with worry. Jack would be back from holiday next week. What was she going to say to him?

Then one day, Polly was watching TV when she thought she heard a faint hissing sound. She turned the TV off and listened.

Yes! There was the sound again. It was coming from near the window.

Polly went over and pulled back one of the curtains. No Doris. And then the hissing stopped.

Polly looked behind the other curtain. There was nothing there. Then she heard the hiss again.

It was coming from Charlie's cage.

He was hissing just like Doris.

This time Polly didn't laugh.

hisssss
hisssss

Mrs McNair came back from her holiday in Spain. She had a present for Polly – a Spanish doll that looked just like the dancer on the postcard.

"Has Charlie been a good boy?" she asked Polly.

"Er ... yes," said Polly.

"Oooeeek! Oooeeek!" said Charlie.

"I've got a new song for you, Charlie," said Mrs McNair. As she carried his cage outside she started to sing, "You and your Spanish eyes," in her funny high voice.

Suddenly she stopped singing and let out a scream.

"What's the matter?" asked Polly.

"A snake!" screamed Mrs McNair. "There's a snake on the doorstep!"

But it wasn't a snake. It was a snake skin.

EEEK!

Chapter 5
Musical Pets

Jack had told Polly about snakes
and their skins. He said that the old
skin sometimes came off and that then
the snake grew a new one. But Polly had
never seen this happen. Now Doris's old
skin was lying on the doorstep. It was
all thin and pale and dry, not the lovely
bright green colour that Doris had been.

Mrs McNair got over her shock and took Charlie home. Polly was glad to see the back of him. She was getting sick of his singing.

"Who cares about Jeannie with the light brown hair?" she said. "It's Doris with the bright green skin that I'm worried about."

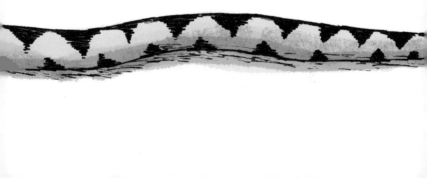

Where was Doris? She must be outside somewhere. Jack had told Polly that snakes didn't like to be cold. They could die if it got too cold. The days had been quite warm and dry, but what about at night?

Polly looked all over the garden, but she couldn't find Doris.

"Have you seen her?" she asked Bill and Ben. And then she had a horrible thought. Snakes ate mice. What if they ate guinea pigs too?

"Mum, we must move Bill and Ben's hutch into the house," she said.

Mum gave an extra loud sigh. "I'm sick of playing musical pets," she said. "Why do we have to keep moving these animals around?"

But Polly wasn't going to take any risks. What if she had to tell Katie that her pets had been eaten by an escaped snake?

It hadn't rained for a few days and the fish pond next door needed filling up. As Polly walked into the greenhouse to get the hose she tried not to think about the fact that Jack was coming back from his holiday the next day.

There were two hoses coiled up side by side in the greenhouse. That was odd. Polly was sure there had only been one last time.

One of the hoses was shorter and fatter than the other one, and it had some black markings on it.

It was rather an odd hose.

In fact, it wasn't a hose at all.

It was Doris!

Chapter 6

Oooeeek!
Oooeeek!

Jack came round the next day with another thank-you present for Polly. It was a book about spiders.

"Has Doris been good?" he asked.

"Er, yes ... very good," said Polly. She showed Jack the old skin, but she didn't tell him anything else.

The evening before Katie was due back, Mum gave Polly two carrots to feed to the guinea pigs. Thin Bill was standing at the front of the hutch going, "Oooeeek! Oooeeek! Oooeeek!" But where was Ben? He was always so greedy, and he had got fatter than ever over the holidays.

"Oh no! Don't say Ben's escaped now!" said Polly.

Then she heard a much softer "Oooeeek! Oooeeek!" noise. At least it couldn't be Charlie this time. He was safely back home with Mrs McNair.

The noise seemed to be coming from the back of the hutch. Very gently, Polly took out some of the hay. Yes, there was Ben. But the soft "oooeeeks" weren't coming from him.

Polly took out some more hay.

There, cuddled up to Ben, were four baby guinea pigs. So that was why Ben had looked so fat!

Chapter 7

Jeannie with the Light Brown Hair

Katie came back from her holidays looking very brown.

"Have Bill and Ben been good?" she asked.

"Yes," said Polly. "But I've got something to show you."

Katie was very excited when she saw the baby guinea pigs. But she said, "Ben doesn't sound right for a mother guinea pig. I'll have to give her a new name. I know – Jen!"

Katie's thank-you present for Polly was a little box made of shells.

Polly liked all her presents – but the best one was still to come. When the baby guinea pigs were old enough to leave their mum, Katie asked if Polly would like to have one of them.

Polly asked Mum. "Oh, go on, Mum, please!" she said.

To her surprise, Mum said, "I'll think about it."

It was a little girl guinea pig. Polly called her Jeannie – because she had light brown hair.

Our books are tested
for children and young people by
children and young people.

Thanks to everyone who consulted on
a manuscript for their time and effort in
helping us to make our books better
for our readers.